The BEST *Hawaiian Style* MOTHER GOOSE Ever!

Hawai'i's version of 14 very popular verses

Written by Kevin Sullivan
Illustrated by Deb Aoki

In memory of Val

Thanks Mom, Dad, K.J., and Aloha
-Kevin Sullivan

Thanks to Mom and Grandma, who always read to me,
and gave me a lifelong love of books.
-Deb Aoki

Other products from **HAWAYA Inc.**

Books:

Return of the Dead Gecko

The Winged Tiger's World Peace Party Puzzle Book

Old MacDonald Hawaiian Style: Auntie Lulu Has a Zoo

Tape:

The Best Hawaiian Style Mother Goose Sing-Along Songs Ever!

(Music by Roslyn Freitas. Vocals by Stephanie Conching)

If you would like information on our other books and tapes, or would like to be on our mailing list, please write to:
HAWAYA
P.O. Box 300
Kailua, HI 96734
E-mail: ksullivn@yahoo.com

Sullivan, Kevin P.,1965-
The Best Hawaiian Style Mother Goose Ever/Kevin Sullivan; Illustrated by Deb Aoki. -- 1st ed.

Summary: Fourteen of the most popular Mother Goose rhymes rewritten "Hawaiian Style."

ISBN: 0-9644149-0-2
(1. Mother Goose - Fiction. 2. Hawaii - Fiction 3. Nursery Rhymes - Fiction)
 Fifth printing - 2002

Printed in Hong Kong.

PRONUNCIATION OF HAWAIIAN WORDS

The Hawaiian alphabet has twelve letters:
A, **E**, **H**, **I**, **K**, **L**, **M**, **N**, **O**, **P**, **U**, and **W**.

Consonants **H**, **K**, **L**, **M**, **N**, and **P** have the same pronunciation in English. **W** is sometimes pronounced like **V**.

Vowels: **A**, **E**, **I**, **O**, and **U**.

A like "a" in "star"

E like "e" in "pet"

I like in "y" in "city"

O like "o" in "gold"

U like "oo" in "moon"

Go Go Gecko

(Baa Baa Black Sheep)

Go, Go, Gecko,
Have you any spots?
Oh, yes, oh, yes,
Quite a lot;

Some on my ʻōpū,
Some on my toes,
And some tiny
yellow ones,

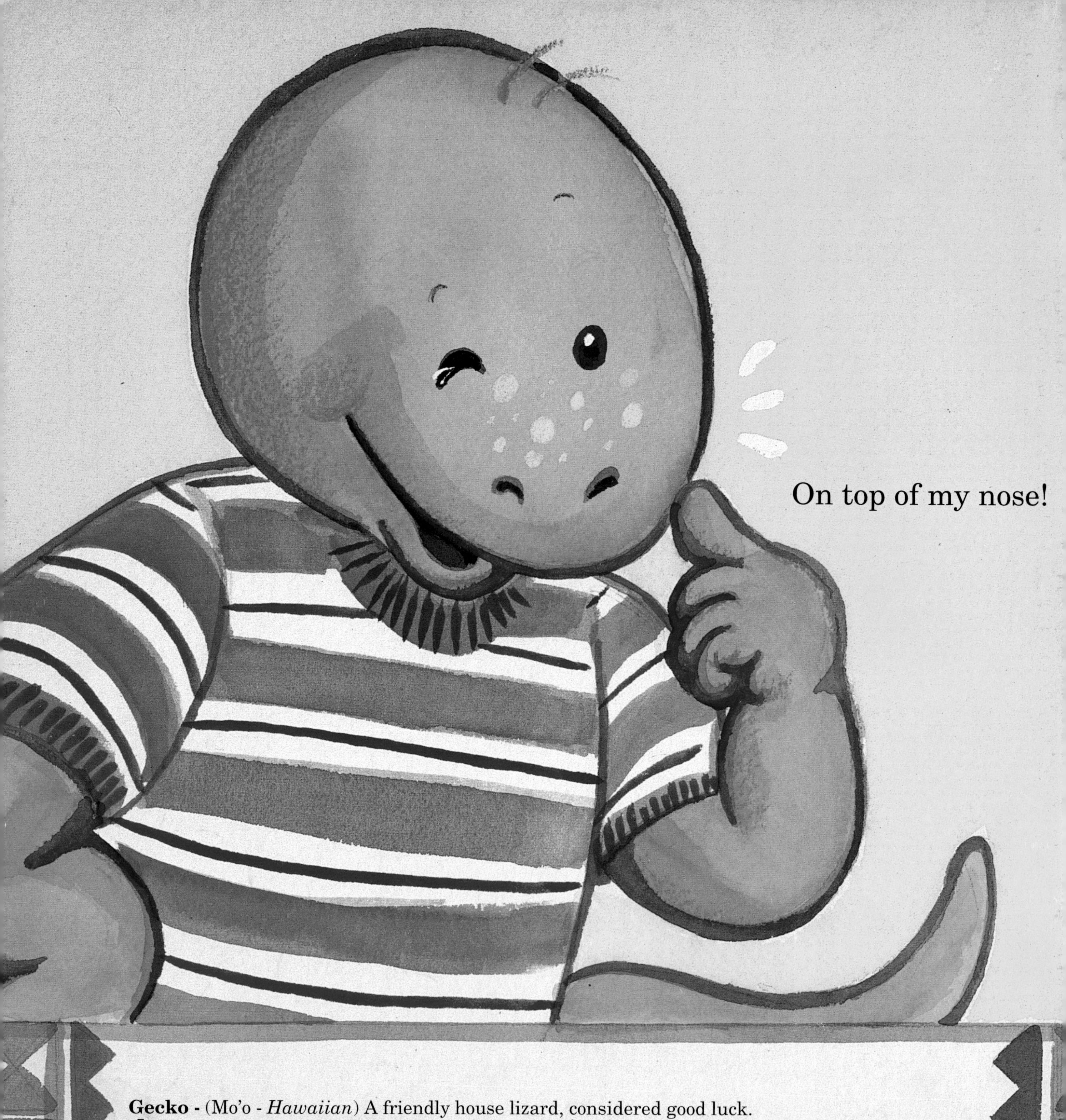

On top of my nose!

Gecko - (Mo'o - *Hawaiian*) A friendly house lizard, considered good luck.
'Ōpū - (*Hawaiian*) Belly, stomach.

Mele Had a Humpback Whale

(Mary Had a Little Lamb)

Mele had a humpback whale,
Its size was great you know;
And everytime they went
somewhere,

Its spout was sure to blow!

Mele - (*Hawaiian*) "Mary"
Humpback Whale - (Koholā - *Hawaiian*) A kind of whale that visits Hawaiian waters from November through April, to nurse its young.

Keaka Jumps High

(Jack Be Nimble)

Keaka jumps high,
Keaka jumps low,
Keaka jumped over

The volcano!

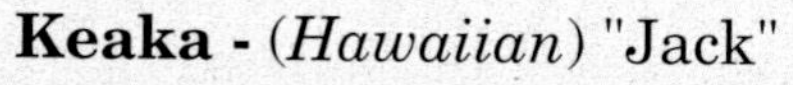

Keaka - (*Hawaiian*) "Jack"
Volcano - A mountain formed by the buildup of lava, or molten rock. The Hawaiian Islands are peaks of large undersea volcanos, and a currently active volcano, Mauna Loa, is on the Big Island of Hawaii.

Mele Mele 'Ukulele

(Mary Mary Quite Contrary)

Mele, Mele, 'Ukulele,
How do your flowers fair?
With fresh maile and pīkake,

And a hibiscus in my hair.

Mele - (*Hawaiian*) "Mary" or a song or chant.
'Ukulele - (*Hawaiian*) "Leaping flea." A four stringed instrument, like a small guitar.
Maile - (*Hawaiian*) Vines of shiny green and fragrant leaves used for garlands (*lei*, *Hawaiian*).
Pīkake - (*Hawaiian*) Jasmine plant, produces small, white fragrant flowers used for leis.
Hibiscus - The Hawaii State Flower. A large, colorful blossom used in decorations.

Kila and Keaka

(Jack and Jill)

Kila and Keaka
Went up Haleakalā
To go for a tī-leaf slide.

From the top,
They didn't stop,
And had a wonderful ride!

Kila - *(Hawaiian)* "Jill" **Keaka -** (*Hawaiian*) "Jack"
Haleakalā - (*Hawaiian*) "House of the Sun." Located on the island of Maui, Haleakalā is one of the largest dormant, or inactive volcanos in the world. Its slopes and crater are home to the rare silversword plant, and to families of nēnē geese. The nēnē goose is the Hawaii State Bird.
Tī-Leaf Slide - An ancient Hawaiian game. Children sat on the large tī (*kī, Hawaiian*) leaves and slid down hills.

Tūtū On a Slipper

(Old Woman Who Lived in a Shoe)

On a rubber slipper, there lived a tūtū.
She had so many children;
Now tell me, what would you do?
It was quite nice, since they paid no rent,
Although once in a while,

Their house up and went.

Rubber Slippers - (a.k.a. zoris, flip flops) Casual footwear in Hawai'i.
Tūtū - (*Hawaiian*, slang) Variation of "kūkū;" usually refers to a grandmother or godmother.

Lōlō Mo'o

(Little Bo Peep)

Lōlō Mo'o lost her rainbow,
And doesn't know where to find her;
Wait for the rain,
And she'll come again,

Sharing her colorful splendor.

Lōlō - (*Hawaiian*) Crazy, dim-witted, or silly.
Mo'o - (*Hawaiian*) A lizard, or reptile of any kind. (i.e. a gecko is a mo'o)
Rainbow - A colorful arch of light created by the sunlight and water vapor, usually appearing after it rains. Hawai'i is home to many rainbows.

Shark Boy

(Jack Sprat)

Shark Boy, he ate no poi,
His sister ate no fish.
But they were so hungry,
You see,

They even ate the dish!

Shark - (Manō, *Hawaiian*) A fierce marine predator, with a tough skin and many rows of teeth. Sharks were often considered to be sacred or worthy of great respect as an *ʻaumakua*, or family guardian spirit.
Poi - (*Hawaiian*) A Hawaiian staple food made from mashed cooked taro (*kalo*, *Hawaiian*) root.

Leilani Lū'au

(Little Miss Muffet)

Leilani Lū'au,
She ate a laulau,
Near a coconut tree.
A wee spider dropped in,
On a thread very thin,

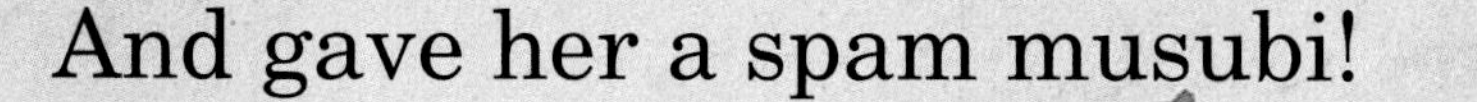

And gave her a spam musubi!

Leilani - (*Hawaiian*) A given name for a girl, means "Heavenly Lei."
Lū'au - (*Hawaiian*) A Hawaiian feast. **Laulau** - (*Hawaiian*) Pork, or chicken, with salted fish wrapped in taro leaves. The bundle is wrapped with a tī-leaf and steamed or baked in an *imu*, or traditional Hawaiian underground oven.
Coconut Tree - A tropical palm tree found almost everywhere in Hawaii.
Spam Musubi - A favorite local food. A ball of sticky rice (*musubi*-Japanese) with a slice of spam (canned meat) on top, wrapped with a ribbon of dried seaweed (*nori*).

Hippity Bippity Bop

(Hickory Dickory Dock)

Hippity Bippity Bop
A mongoose in the clock.
The clock rang two,

Mongoose - (Manakuke, *Hawaiian*) A small animal resembling a weasel found on the Hawaiian Islands.
Aloha Tower - Once the tallest building in Honolulu, Aloha Tower is a landmark at Honolulu Harbor.

Hey Mu'u Mu'u

(Hey Diddle Diddle)

Hey Mu'u Mu'u,
The pig and the ipu,
The whale jumped over a star;
The nēnē goose laughed
to see such things,

And the fish drove away in his car!

Mu'u mu'u - (*Hawaiian*) A loose flowing gown, usually with floral prints.
Ipu - (*Hawaiian*) A hollow gourd used as a percussion instrument for Hawaiian songs and chants.
Nēnē - (*Hawaiian*) The Hawaii State Bird. A native Hawaiian goose found on Mauna Loa, on the island of Hawai'i, and Haleakalā, on Maui.

Three Big Pigs

(Three Blind Mice)

Three Big Pigs,
Three Big Pigs.
See how they dance!
See how they dance!
They danced the hula and danced the jig.
Each wore a grass skirt and each wore a wig.

Did you ever see a more crazier gig,
Than three big pigs?

Pigs - (*Pua'a, Hawaiian*) Introduced to the Hawaiian islands by the first Polynesian voyagers. Wild pigs still live in the mountains and forests of the Hawaiian islands.
Hula - (*Hawaiian*) "To dance, or a dance." A graceful Hawaiian dance.

Keiki Keaka

(Little Jack Horner)

Keiki Keaka,
Wore his palaka,
Eating rainbow shave ice.
He put in his spoon,

And finished it soon,
And said, "Now I want
some fried rice!"

Keiki - (*Hawaiian*) A child. **Keaka** - (*Hawaiian*) "Jack"
Palaka - (*Hawaiian*) A Hawaiian plaid pattern material, used in casual wear like shirts, or shorts.
Rainbow shave ice - A deluxe snow cone. Finely shaved ice in a cone, topped with two or more flavors of colorful syrup to resemble a rainbow.
Fried rice - A favorite local food made by frying cooked rice, Portuguese sausage, egg, green onion, and other vegetables. Good for cleaning out the refrigerator.

Tango Mango

(HumptyDumpty)

Tango Mango danced in the breeze,
Tango Mango fell when he sneezed;
All of the mynahs and all of their friends,

Ate pickled mango for weeks without end.

Mango - A sweet and juicy tropical fruit, eaten both green or ripe.
Mynahs - Tropical birds with a sassy walk and squawk.
Pickled mango - Sliced green mangos preserved with a sweet-sour vinegar solution.

GLOSSARY

Aloha Tower - Once the tallest building in Honolulu, Aloha Tower is a Honolulu Harbor landmark.

Coconut Tree - A tropical palm tree found almost everywhere in Hawaii.

Fried Rice - A favorite local food, adapted from traditional Chinese cuisine. Local style fried rice can include Portuguese sausage, green onions, eggs, or other leftover foods. Good for "cleaning out the refrigerator."

Gecko -*(Mo'o - Hawaiian)* A friendly house lizard, considered good luck.

Haleakalā - *(Hawaiian)* "House of the Sun." Located on the island of Maui, Haleakalā is one of the largest dormant, or inactive volcanos in the world. Its slopes and crater are home to the rare silversword plant, and to families of nēnē geese. The nēnē goose is the Hawaii State Bird.

Hibiscus - The Hawaii State Flower. A large colorful blossom used in decorations.

Hula - *(Hawaiian)* "To dance; a dance." A Hawaiian dance.

Humpback Whale - *(Koholā, Hawaiian)* A kind of whale that visits Hawaiian waters from November through April, to nurse its young.

Ipu - *(Hawaiian)* A hollow gourd used as a percussion instrument for Hawaiian songs and chants.

Keaka - (*Hawaiian*) "Jack"

Keiki - (*Hawaiian*) A child.

Kila - *(Hawaiian)* "Jill"

Laulau - *(Hawaiian)* Taro leaves. The bundle is wrapped with a tī-leaf and steamed or baked in an *imu*, or traditional Hawaiian underground oven.

Leilani - *(Hawaiian)* A given name for a girl, meaning "Heavenly Lei."

Lōlō - *(Hawaiian)* Crazy, dim-witted, or silly.

Lu'au - (*Hawaiian*) A Hawaiian feast.

Maile - (*Hawaiian*) Vines of shiny, green and fragrant leaves used for garlands, (Lei, *Hwn.*)

Mango - A sweet and juicy tropical fruit, eaten both green or ripe.

Mele - *(Hawaiian)* "Mary"

Mongoose -*(Manakuke, Hawaiian)* A small animal resembling a weasel found in Hawai'i.

Mo'o -*(Hawaiian)* A lizard, or reptile of any kind. *(i.e. a gecko is a mo'o)*

Mu'u mu'u - *(Hawaiian)* A loose flowing gown, usually with floral prints, worn by women.

Mynahs - Tropical birds with a sassy walk and squawk.

Nēnē- *(Hawaiian)* The Hawaii State Bird. A native Hawaiian goose found on Mauna Loa, on the island of Hawaii, and Haleakalā, on Maui.

'Ōpū -*(Hawaiian)* Belly, stomach.

Palaka (*Hawaiian*) A Hawaiian plaid pattern material, used in casual wear like shirts, or shorts.

Pickled mango - Sliced green mangos preserved with a sweet-sour vinegar solution.

Pigs (Pua'a, *Hawaiian*) Introduced to the Hawaiian islands by the first Polynesian voyagers. Wild pigs still live in the mountains and forests of the Hawaiian islands.

Pīkake - (*Hawaiian*) Jasmine plant, produces small, white fragrant flowers used for leis.

Poi - (*Hawaiian*) A Hawaiian staple food made from mashed cooked taro (*kalo*, Hawaiian) root.

Rainbow - A colorful arch of light created by the sunlight and water vapor, usually appearing after it rains. Hawaii is home to many rainbows.

Rainbow shave ice - A deluxe snow cone. Finely shaved ice packed into a paper cone, topped with two or more flavors of colorful syrup to resemble a rainbow.

Rubber slippers - (a.k.a. zoris, flip flops) Casual footwear in Hawai'i.

Shark- *(Manō-Hawaiian)* A fierce marine predator, with a tough skin and many rows of teeth. Sharks were often considered to be sacred as an *'aumakua*, or family guardian spirit.

Spam Musubi - A favorite local food. A ball of sticky rice *(musubi-Japanese)* with a slice of spam *(canned meat)* on top, and wrapped with a ribbon of dried seaweed (*nori, Japanese*).

Tī Leaf Slide - An ancient Hawaiian game. Children sat on the large tī (*kī-Hawaiian)* leaves and slid down hills.

Tūtū - (Hawaiian, slang) Variation of "kūkū;" usually refers to a grandmother or godmother.

'Ukulele - (*Hawaiian*) "Leaping flea." A four stringed instrument, like a small guitar.

Volcano - A mountain formed by the buildup of lava, or molten rock. The Hawaiian Islands are peaks of large undersea volcanos. A currently active volcano, Mauna Loa, is on the Big Island of Hawai'i.